Drop

Gayathri . K & Sankari. D

All global publishing rights are held by

Ukiyoto Publishing

Published in 2023

Content Copyright © K. Gayathri
Book Designed by Sreelakshmy
ISBN 9789360165758

All rights reserved.
No part of this publication may be reproduced, transmitted, or stored in a retrieval system, in any form by any means, electronic, mechanical, photocopying, recording or otherwise, without the prior permission of the publisher.

The moral rights of the author have been asserted.

This is a work of fiction. Names, characters, businesses, places, events, locales, and incidents are either the products of the author's imagination or used in a fictitious manner. Any resemblance to actual persons, living or dead, or actual events is purely coincidental.

This book is sold subject to the condition that it shall not by way of trade or otherwise, be lent, resold, hired out or otherwise circulated, without the publisher's prior consent, in any form of binding or cover other than that in which it is published.

This title is produced in Association with Pachyderm Tales

www.pachydermtales.com

ACKNOWLEDGEMENT

We whole heartedly thank Mohanasundari Jaganathan, Managing Director of Sharp Electrodes Pvt Ltd for funding this project.

Without her this book would not be possible!

This book was a part of workshop conducted in our college,
NGM College Pollachi and Pachyderm Tales. I whole heartedly thank our management, our teachers and HOD of English Dept, NGM as well as Suja Mam for this initiative.

More than half of our planet is made up of water. Deep within the ocean lived a drop named Tinu .

Tinu loves his home very much, it is so

cool and

colourful

Tinu loves his mother Sangu.

His mother Sangu wakes Tinu and asked, "How did you sleep last night dear?" Tinu said, "I slept good mom, but Mr. Moony was

snoring and his light was in my face".

Tinu's mom laughed and said that Moony was a noisy sleeper. Sangu asked Tinu to go on a trip.

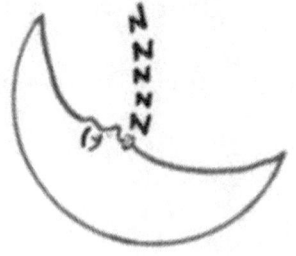

Tinu suddenly realised that today was the first day of school.

Tinu remembered the tales narrated by his brother elder - drops were scared to leave the comfort of the ocean .

Tinu said, **"No Mumma, I will never leave you and my lovely home."**

Sangu was worried about her son Tinu and that time, there came a sea octopus near Sangu and enquired, "Why are you looking sad, is there is any problem?" Sangu spoke about the school and Tinu's fear towards the school.

Octopus talked to **Tinu** about the importance of going to school and after hearing this **Tinu** accepted to go to school.

In any case his mother **Sangu** still felt

Sad.

Sunny was the principle of the school. Sunny called Cloudy to pickup the drops from ocean to the school.

Cloudy came near the sea and call

out the name list of students.

Cloudy picked up and they started to travel in the sky. **Tinu** was afraid because of **Cloudy's** speed!

Tinu said to **Cloudy**, "Can you float a little slow?"

"No, I can't do that I have other pickups on the way and we are already late," said **Cloudy**.

Tinu said, "Okay." **Cloudy** Picked - Up many other drops for school and once every body was on board **Cloudy** got heavy!

Cloudy asked help from **Windy** to blow with full force to carry **Cloudy** to wherever he had to float .

Drop   19

Cloudy dropped all the drops at their stops some on the mountains, some on the green grass, some on the human house but before the **Cloudy** could reach the right stop he was pushed by another Harsh Wind .

Drop 21

Cloudy and the **Harsh Wind** started to argue with each other causing

thunders that made

Tinu to fall from Cloudy.

Tinu fell on a dry forest. In the forest the water level was very low due to the lack of rain.

Many animals were affected by it and were eagerly waiting for the rain drops to fall upon them.

In the field, the humans planted the seeds to grow but there was no rain drop, so they felt very bad!

If the plants did not grow they will neither

food and money for their daily living...

After seeing the situation of animals and humans **Tinu** thought about helping the people!

So **Tinu** called **Cloudy** to help him. **Cloudy** came there and picked-up the drop to its own sea land.

Tinu got into the sea and spoke about the people's situation. **Tinu** gathered all his friends in the sea, then all of them started to help him.

Cloudy picked up all the drop sand sent them to the forest. **Cloudy** dropped the drops in the forest as a rain!

Drop

The neem tree on seeing the cloud, Happily exclaimed," Ahh! It's Raining!"

All the birds and animals welcomed the drops and they were very happy!

In the forest rainwater level was increasing and all the animals and humans are happy and praised the rain drops and they were thanking the rain drops.

The raindrops soaked the soil making the roots healthy, made the tress greener and bigger, made the fresh grass grow as crops began to grow.

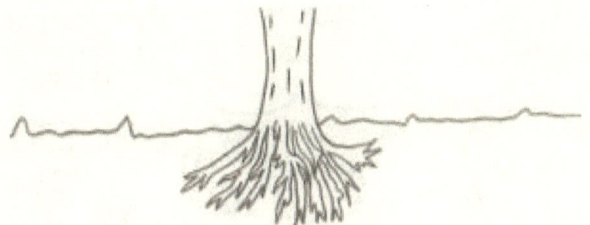

The rain drops gave the forest a gorgeous renewal of life and happiness. The rain drops flowed happily and one day they reached the greatest expanse of water and there they reached the mighty ocean again.

After reaching home, **Tinu** recited this **great tale** to his mother and told her how he had made many living beings happy and healthy.

He promised his mother that he would always attend to his responsibilities and be the reason for joy among the world.

Sangu felt so proud of her son after listening to him.

Again, all the drops were away with Mr. Cloudy to **explore** the world as rain Drops.

This never- ending process of evaporation is the best recycling process in the world.

Save water! Save life!

The Author

The story 'Drop' is the first published book by Gayathri Kalimuthu, who is pursuing her BA English literature at NGM college. She is an innovative writer and artist. Her goal is to remind the world and our next-generation about the importance of water and its sustainability through her writings. Her family, friends, and her zest to make an impact on people drives her forward to achieve her ambitions.

The Illustrator

Sankari, the illustrator of this book loves to draw pictures and she has made it her hobby. Drawing is her only way to handle her emotions and ensure that her inner feelings comes out in the best foot outside. Dancing and singing are her other hobbies. Despite being a creative artist, she intends to spend her life as a teacher.

www.ingramcontent.com/pod-product-compliance
Lightning Source LLC
LaVergne TN
LVHW041639070526
838199LV00052B/3462